THE
KNICKERS

...AS ALLAN

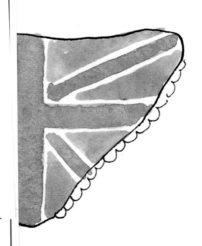

RED FOX

To Jenny

A RED FOX BOOK : 978 0 099 41314 1

This Red Fox edition published 2000

11

Red Fox Books are published by Random House Children's Books,
61-63 Uxbridge Road, London W5 5SA,
a division of The Random House Group Ltd,
in Australia by Random House Australia (Pty) Ltd,
20 Alfred Street, Milsons Point, Sydney, NSW 2061, Australia
in New Zealand by Random House New Zealand Ltd,
18 Poland Road, Glenfield, Auckland 10, New Zealand
and in South Africa by Random House (Pty) Ltd,
Isle of Houghton, Corner of Boundary Road & Carse O'Gowrie, Houghton 2198, South Africa

THE RANDOM HOUSE GROUP Limited Reg No. 954009
www.kidsatrandomhouse.co.uk

www.nicholasallan.co.uk

A CIP catalogue record for this book is available from the British Library.

Printed in China

The Queen likes to dress smartly.

So she has an enormous wardrobe for her clothes...

...and a slightly smaller chest of drawers for all her knickers.

Dilys looks after the Queen's knickers.

She has a special trunk for when the Queen goes away.

One day the trunk went *missing*!

It caused a great crisis...

...and was only *just* sorted out before it reached the NEWS AT TEN.

The trunk had got mixed up...

...with a picnic hamper.

ROYAL WEDDINGS

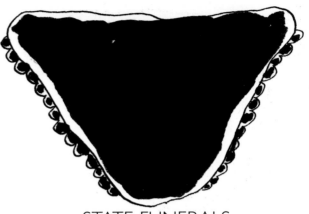

STATE FUNERALS

HORSE RIDING
(WITH EXTRA PADDING)

FOREIGN VISITS

The Queen has knickers

KNICKER GUIDE

GARDEN PARTIES

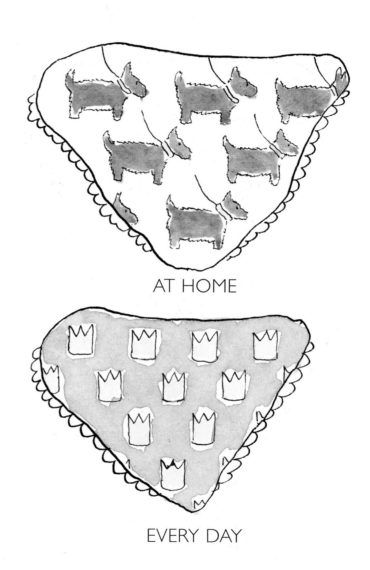

AT HOME

BALMORAL (WOOLLEN)

EVERY DAY

for all occasions.

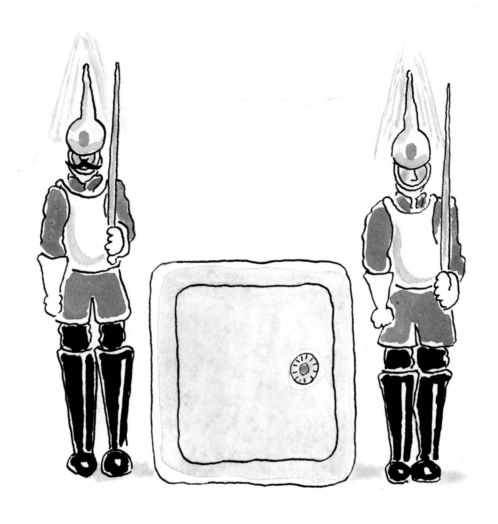

At the opening of Parliament
the Queen wears her VIP's (Very Important Pair).
There is no picture of these. But here is the safe
where they're locked up with other state secrets.

When she travels
she has special knickers with a small
parachute inside them...

...just in case.

(She has another pair for

when she's on board ship.)

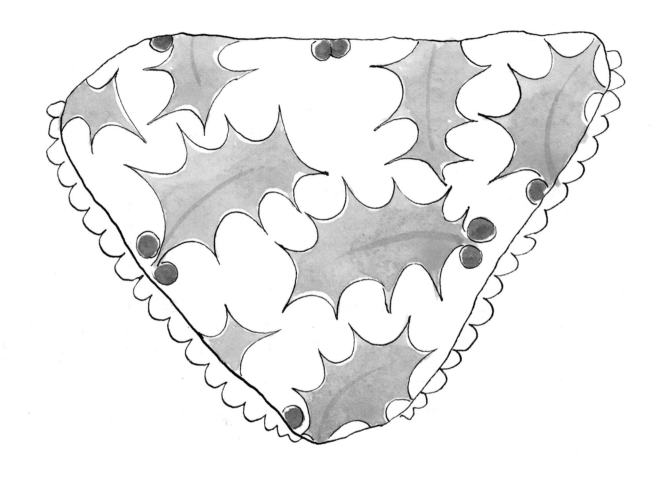

But her most special knickers
are her Christmas knickers.
They are a gift from Scandinavia and are traditionally
decorated with real holly...

...which is why
she keeps her Christmas
message very short.

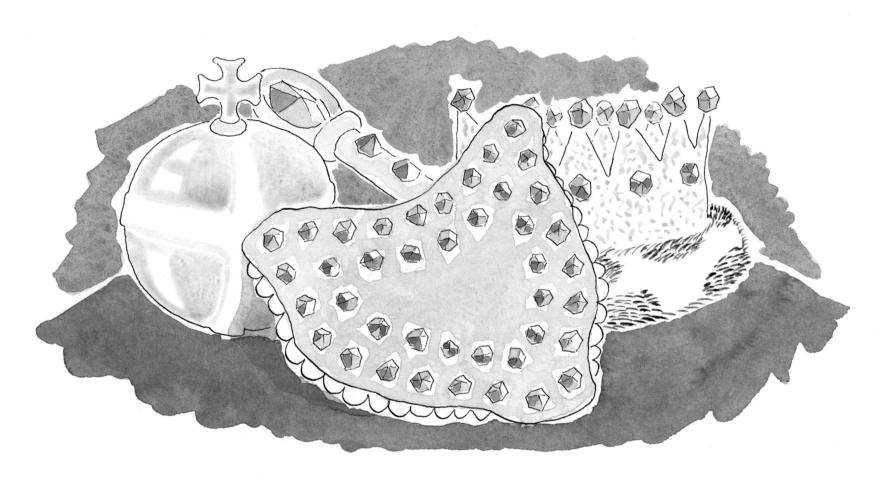

The Royal Knickers, though, are her most
valuable. They are made of pure silk
with gold thread and encrusted with
diamonds, emeralds and rubies.

They were first worn
by Queen Victoria and are
rather baggy.

I wonder what knickers the Queen would wear
if she visited our school?

There'd be a *terrific* flap at the Palace.

'Call the Royal Knicker-maker, Dilys!'

'I shall just have to wear my "Every Day" knickers.'

Then the poor Queen would feel very awkward,
as she's so particular about her clothes.

But I would tell her something to put her at ease.
'Don't worry about your knickers,
Your Majesty,' I'd whisper.
'You see, *no one can see them anyway.*'

Then she'd be sure to send a special note
to me afterwards by the Royal Mail saying:

*'Her Majesty wishes
to inform you that her
visit was most enjoyable...
and very comfortable.'*